A First-Start® Easy Reader

This easy reader contains only 51 different words, repeated often to help the young reader develop word recognition and interest in reading.

Basic word list for *A Bath for a Beagle:*

a	dog	car
are	dirt	now
is	dirty	Burton
of	need	beagle
on	needs	does
in	bath	likes
out	bathtub	where
off	here	under
our	house	run
he	roll	wet
he's	rolling	soap
we	jump	hose
to	jumps	shakes
the	come	dries
by	clean	cellar
this	but	splashes
not	his	bushes

A Bath for a Beagle

Written by Thomas Crawford

Illustrated by Veronica Buffington

Troll Associates

This
is our
dog,
Burton.

Burton is a beagle.

He likes to run.

He likes to jump.

He likes to roll in the dirt.

Burton is dirty.

Burton needs
a bath.

Here is the bathtub.

Here is
the hose.

Here is the soap.

Where is Burton?

He's not in his house.

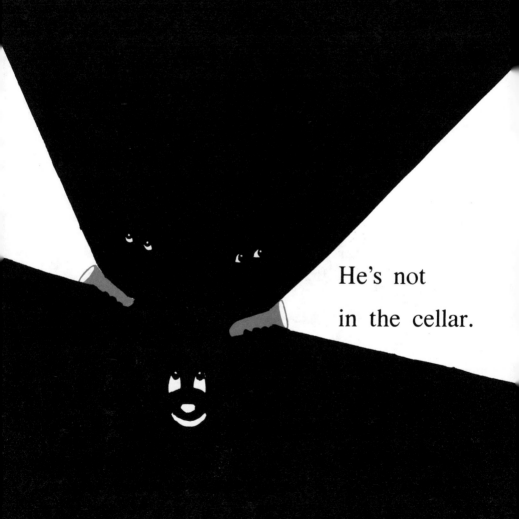

He's not
in the cellar.

He's not in the bushes.

He's under the car.

Come on, Burton.
Jump in.

Burton splashes.

Burton shakes.

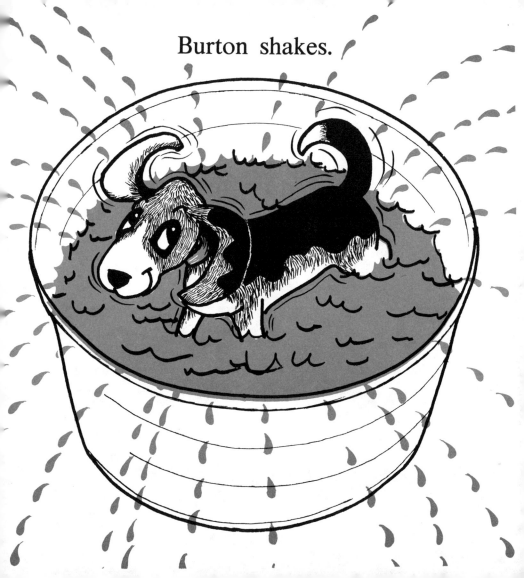

Now Burton is clean.

But we
are
wet.

Burton jumps
out of the
bathtub.

Burton dries off
by rolling in the dirt.

Does Burton
need a
bath
now?